I0526905

Copyright 2024 Randy Spohn, All Rights Reserved

Illustrated by Madeline Jonker.

No part of this book may be reproduced, stored in a retrieval system, or transmitted by any means without the written permission of the author.

Published by White Feather Press. (www.whitefeatherpress.com)

ISBN 978-1-61808-220-6

Printed in the United States of America

White Feather Press

Reaffirming Faith in God, Family and Country

Lonnie the Lizard and the Deep Woods

Written by
Randy Spohn

Illustrated by
Madeline Jonker

About the Author

Randy is a military retiree of 26 years, serving in the Army. Spohn is a substitute teacher in the Allegan County school district in Michigan. He has been married for 45 years to his wonderful wife, Sue. Randy became interested in writing children's books when he saw the struggles children have with reading and writing. His goal is to allow children to enjoy reading and learning life lessons of being polite, courteous and responsible with their choices. These books are for any age who enjoys a good story, a peaceful journey though a day with a lizard and a good laugh.

About the Illustrator

Madeline Jonker is an 16 year old artist and illustrator. Her first illustrated book is Lonnie the Lizard. Her passion for art began during the lockdown of 2020. Madeline lives in Hastings Michigan with her parents, sister, her dog Luna, and her cat Ariel. She paints and after High school she wants to become a graphic designer.

Lonnie and his family

Lonnie lived in a tree deep inside the forest with his mother, father and 9 sisters and brothers. His brothers and sisters had names that all started with the letter "L". There was Larry, Lester, Lidia, Lolita, Legend, Linda, Logan, Laura, and Lindsey. Lonnie was the youngest.

Get ready kids! Lonnie the Lizard is ready for more adventure.

So hurry up and turn the page to find out what happens next!

It was another sunny day by the stream. Lonnie and his family were having a picnic by the water and enjoying the sound of the crickets, which they loved to eat, and the bugs in the air.

You see, lizards did not need to pack their picnic lunch. They just sat in the open air and watched for their meals to arrive by air, water, or land.

Soon after they had eaten all the bugs they could find, the boys Lonnie, Logan and Legend decided to go into the Deep Woods and find some bigger bugs to eat. For some reason the crickets and moths just did not fill them up. They wanted to find something for dessert.

On the way, Lonnie asked his brothers what they were looking for. Lonnie was the youngest so he did not have much experience in the woods. "Hey, what do we look for and what do whatever we are looking for look like?"

Legend turned to one side and looked Lonnie in the face. "We are looking for food. Any bug that looks delicious and inviting."

"Ya" chimed in Logan, "Anything that looks delicious and inviting." The two brothers just shook their heads as if the question Lonnie asked was dumb. Of course, he knew, no questions were dumb. His dad always said, there aren't any dumb questions except the question that isn't asked.

Soon the lizards were deep into the woods. Deeper than they had ever gone. As they walked, they saw a tree with a large vine on it. "Hey, remember the vine we climbed on the other side of the creek?"

"That had that round thing we ate that was very tasty. Maybe this vine has some for all of us," suggested Lonnie.

The lizard brothers thought about this. Finally, Legend suggested to Lonnie that he climb first. After all, it was his idea.

"Well, OK," said Lonnie. He was not sure this was a good idea, but had to climb now since he did suggest it. Up he started to climb. It was easy at first. The vine was very large, but the higher he got, the skinner the vine got. He found himself hanging on tighter and tighter until he was afraid to take his hand off the vine.

As Lonnie looked down, he did not realize how high he was. "Hey Guys! I'm scared. How do I get down?" Lonnie was almost crying he was so scared.

"Scared? I knew you would do this," said Logan. "Do you see any of those juicy round things up there? I'm hungry and I did not come all the way out here to go away hungry."

Lonnie looked around him, "Not up here. I'm not sure how I am going to get down. Can you guys come up here and get me?"

Now his brothers were getting scared. How in the world would they rescue Lonnie out of that tree? They did not want to climb up there. On the other hand, they couldn't leave Lonnie stuck up in the tree. What would Dad say?

Legend and Logan thought and thought. They looked around for a long stick, but nothing they found was long enough. Maybe a long skinny vine to throw up to Lonnie. Nah, they could not throw that high. Their arms were too short.

Lonnie looked around him. He was holding on tight, but started to get a little less scared. His tummy was rumbling now. He was starting to get hungry again, and all he could think about was food, and how to get down and get some more food.

As he looked around, he noticed a branch hanging down just out of reach. He would need to take a couple more steps higher to allow him to reach the limb. Once he got to the limb, he wondered if he could turn himself around and climb down the vine headfirst.

He had to take a chance. His brothers were no help. As he took another step up the vine, he felt the vine move which made him stop. Just one more step and he would be there. Finally, he was able to grab the branch.

He turned himself around and started down the vine. As he began his climb to the ground, his feet started to slip, and he was soon sliding down the vine.

"Hey, here I come!" Lonnie said with excitement. The ride down was fun. He had never gone this fast down a tree before.

As Lonnie got to the bottom of the vine, the vine took a twist upward. Lonnie few into the air then came down in a pile of leaves.

"Man, you guys need to try this. That was fun." expressed Lonnie to Legend and Logan.

They both looked at him like he was crazy. "I don't know, should we?" Legend said to Logan.

"Come on. You guys' chicken? Just climb to the branch, turn around and slide down. It's fun!" said Lonnie.

Legend ran to the vine ahead of Logan. Up, up and up he went. Once he got to the hanging branch, Legend turned himself around. At first, he was scared but if Lonnie could do it, so could Legend. He turned himself around, looking down at Logan and Lonnie on the ground. He took a deep breath and let his grip soften. Soon Legend was sliding down the vine. Faster and faster he went, until, he too, hit the bottom of the vine and then the upward turn. In the air flew Legend, laughing as he was airborne. He hit the pile of leaves and was so excited, he was on his feet with the first bounce.

Logan took his turn and was filled with just as much fun and excitement as the others. Soon, they were taking turns up and down the vine. All the while forgetting, they went into the Deep Woods to find food. Soon the lizards were tired.

"Time for us to head home," said Legend.

"Yep, I am tired," responded Logan.

"Man, am I hungry," Lonnie said as he was rubbing his stomach.

As the lizard brothers arrived at home, they had a good laugh, sitting around the log with their brothers and sisters.

Their parents brought out some bug juice and gummy worms. Laughter filled the Lizard's log. Soon, the three brothers were in bed.

"That was a great day. We need to go into the Deep Woods again," yawned Lonnie.
Soon they were fast asleep......zzzzzz

Coming Soon!

More adventures

of Lonnie the Lizard

www.ingramcontent.com/pod-product-compliance
Lightning Source LLC
Chambersburg PA
CBHW041543240626
47164CB00002B/107